I0626368

Copyright © 2020 by Allen Isom

All rights reserved. No part of this book may be
reproduced or used in any manner without written permission on
the copyright owner except for the use of quotations in a book
review.

ISBN 978-1-7356519-0-3

I'd like to dedicate this book to my wife, Nikki.
Without her constructive criticism and constant encouragement
I would have never finished this book.

And to my two sons William and Jacob for just being
incredibly supportive and helping me take care of their mom
while I worked on this.

And finally, all the other family and friends who didn't get
mentioned by name. Thanks for all your help and listening to me
go on and on about making this book for eight or so years.

Table of Contents

Table of Contents

Wretched Little Book

There's a monster in my closet, but I'm too afraid to look.
So I'll keep writing poems in my wretched little book.
Now, if the day should find me alive and still unshook,
Then I'll sit here, for love of fear, and read my wretched book.

Finding Peace

To sleep and dream sweet,
an escape from the sadness.
The sleepless dream not,
but find peace in madness.

Burn The Witch

They burned me at the stake for the God I had rejected.
Also, for the souls of all the children I collected.
But, covering my mouth was something they neglected.
'Twas quite the oversight and I cursed them, as expected.

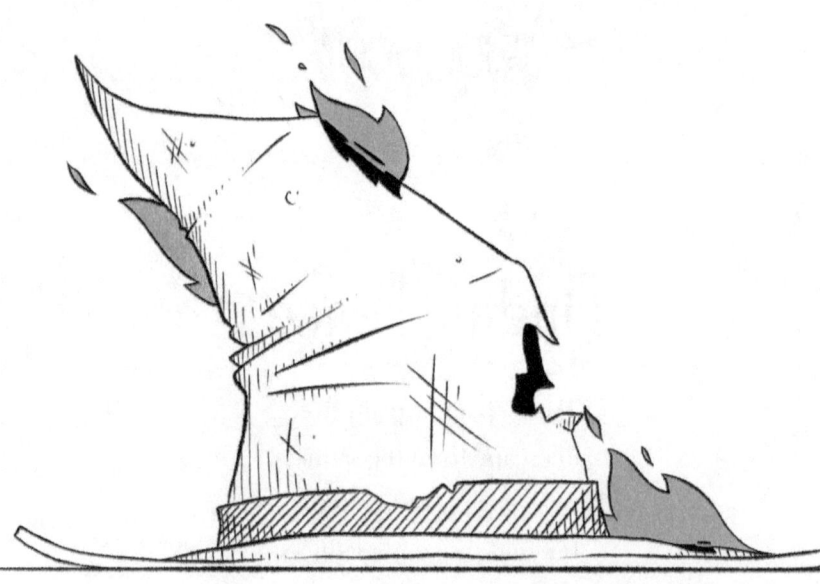

The Deadwoods

Deep in the gloom, 'neath the deadwood trees,
The dead come alive and do as they please.

Through the whirling wind and the bubbling mud,
Come occasional screams and splattering blood.

Few people enter, and fewer survive,
They either go mad or get eaten alive.

The signs posted up read, "DANGER AHEAD!"
So, don't mind the signs if you don't mind the dead.

Creeping Death

You'll find it in the darkness, but clearer in the day.
And though you may ignore it, it never goes away.

You knew that it was coming. You watched it all along.
But every day, in every way, you wanted to be wrong.

In every single smile now, or dare to laugh at all,
Your memories are poisoned - or at least what you recall.

And when you think it's better, if only for a day,
It eagerly reminds you that it hasn't gone away.

The creeping death won't kill you, but know it surely could.
Even when you're happy, it will make you wish it would.

C'est la Vie

Forgive me, my dear, as you tremble with fear,
Some patience now as we proceed.

For each day that I live, there is more to forgive,
With every goddamnedable deed.

Now, the real problem here isn't anger or fear,
But it's simply my lack of remorse.

I'm not sorry, nor torn, it's just how I was born,
And my killing you's par for the course.

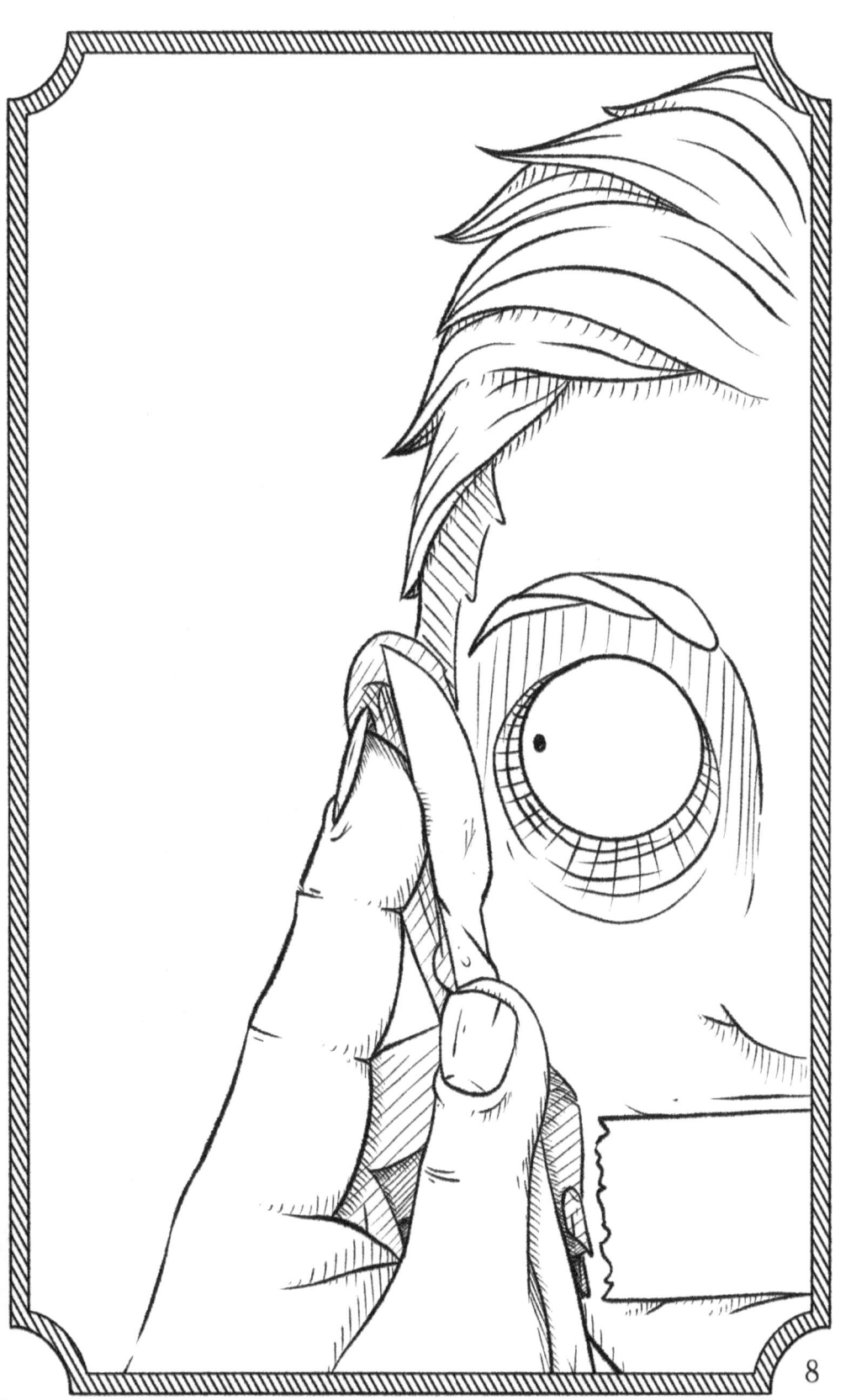

8

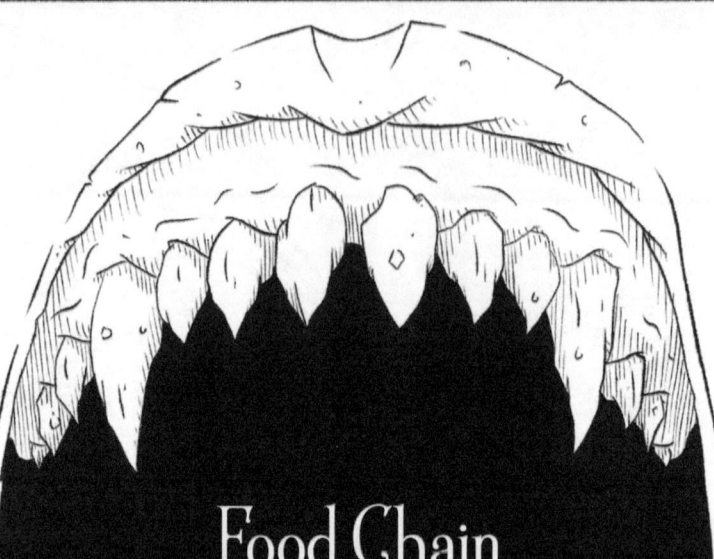

Food Chain

I'm the monster they say as their teeth grind on meat.
Yet they all kill and slaughter if only to eat.

"Stop it," they beg, "Please let us live!"
But their blood is too good, and they've so much to give.

"You could eat something else. Please, give it a try!"
But they haven't gone vegan, so then why should I?

The Dead Ones

As dead leaves fall on chiseled stone
On hallowed ground and rotted bone
On loved ones gone we can't atone
Beneath the pale moon.

The dead ones laugh because they're dead
With not a worry in their head
But you should feel naught but dread
For you shall join them soon.

Smiles Everyone

All I see are smiling faces
Every single place I go.

And though this town is small,
I'm the person they all know.

And though it's not a contest,
I'm the one they like the best.

Even those who visit
Learn to smile like the rest.

12

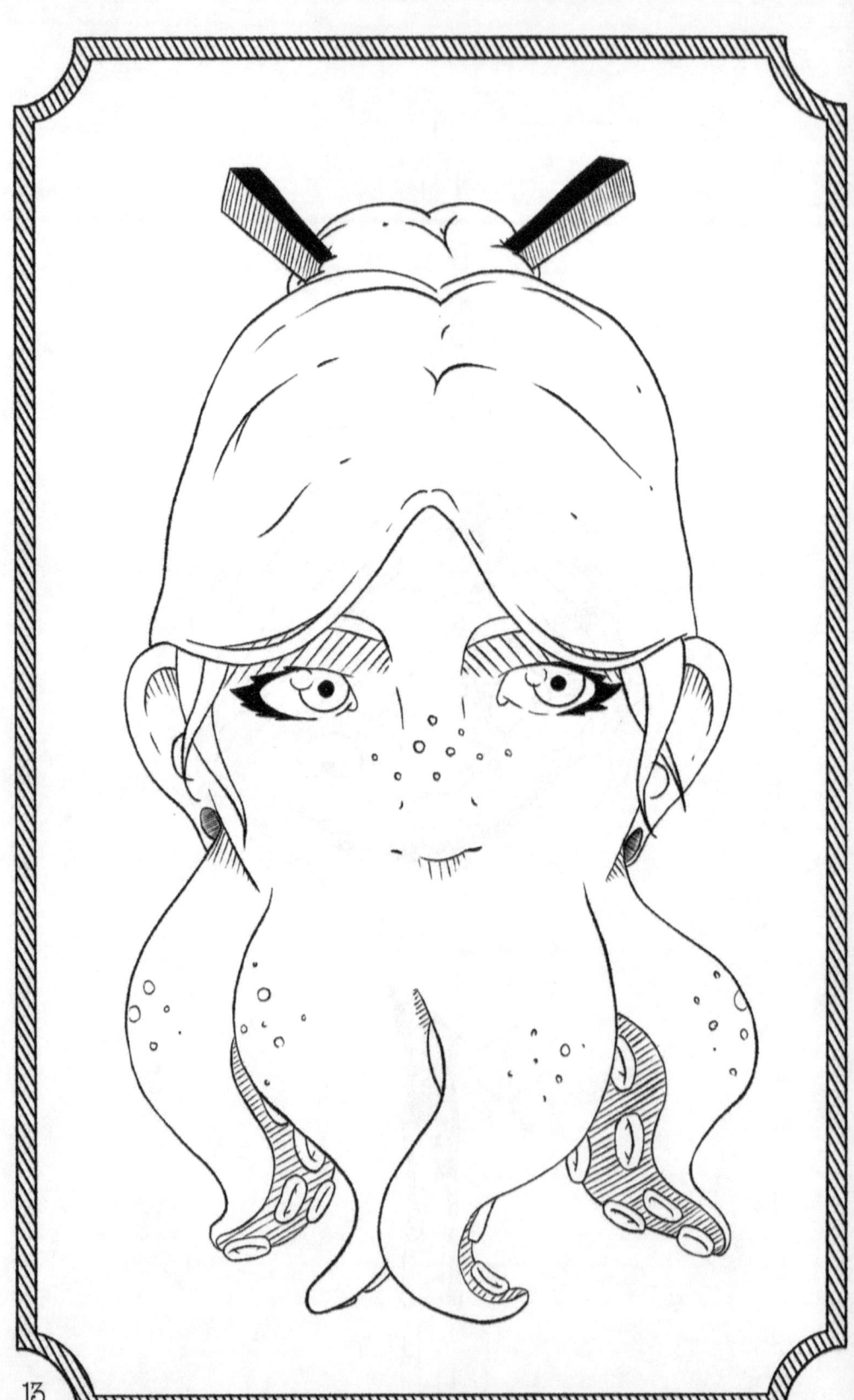

Squid Face Girl

On half of her face, the tentacles curled,
And made Kali feel alone in the world.
She'd never known love, and she'd never been kissed.
Oh, all the things her poor squid face missed.

At school they were mean, what they said and they did,
So she always ran home, all alone, where she hid.
In a little old room, in a little old city,
She sat there alone. From her parents; no pity.

One day, it so happened, she received an invite
To a party that took place one Saturday night.
So, against her own instincts, she went to have fun.
Once there, she discovered, for her there'd be none.

She was pushed in a closet, a room dark as night.
She could feel another closed in with her tight.
Seven minutes, for her, an unbearable trick.
As for the poor boy, it just made him feel sick.

So, she'll carry on living, well at least for now,
And keep up the hope - though she isn't sure how
One day she'll find kindness or, heaven forbid,
a person who can find the beauty in squid.

Dream Come True

Janet found a genie who could make one wish come true.
So, Janet took her time so she could really think it through.

Should she wish for a castle, or a pony she could race?
Should she wish to be an astronaut exploring outer space?

Maybe she would simply wish to have a brand new doll.
Oh this was tough, with just one wish, how could she have it all?

Then it finally dawned on her, "I wish my dreams came true!"
The genie smiled, for he knew exactly what to do.

That night Janet had a dream that was awfully bad.
Her mom became a monster, then gobbled up her dad.

When Janet finally woke, into her parents room she sped,
And there upon the floor, right by the door, was daddy's head.

Then Janet cried out for her mom, who suddenly appeared.
But her mother was a monster, just as Janet feared.

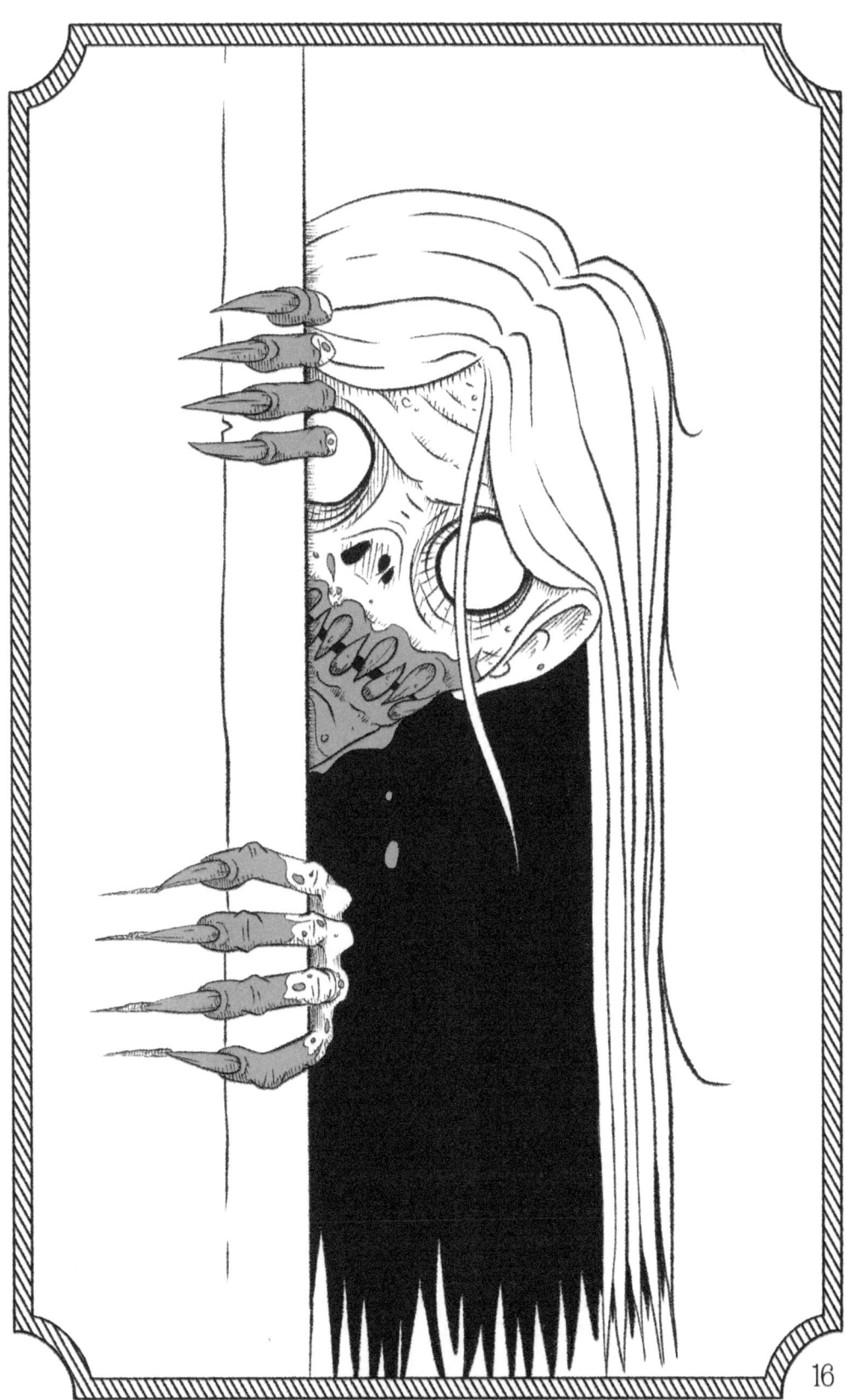

16

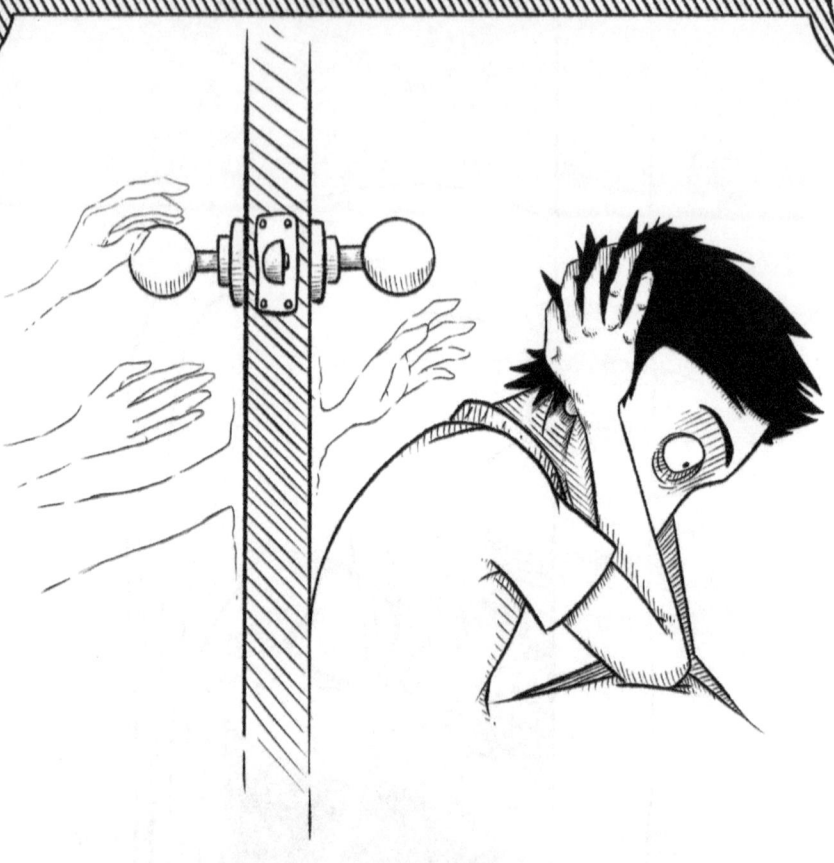

Yet They Linger

I killed them. I admit it.

I killed the good and dead.

Though I did not expect they'd go on living in my head.

I killed them, like I said,

And I'd kill 'em all some more.

Even as they come a knocking right outside my door.

I killed them; yes it's true.

And I'm sure I did it right.

If so, how come I have to kill them every single night?

The Damned

Marionettes. My little pets.
Dance your dance for me.

Hollow things, up on your strings.
Blind; you cannot see.

Follow me. You're only free
To choose as I command.

One by one, my will be done.
For all of you are damned.

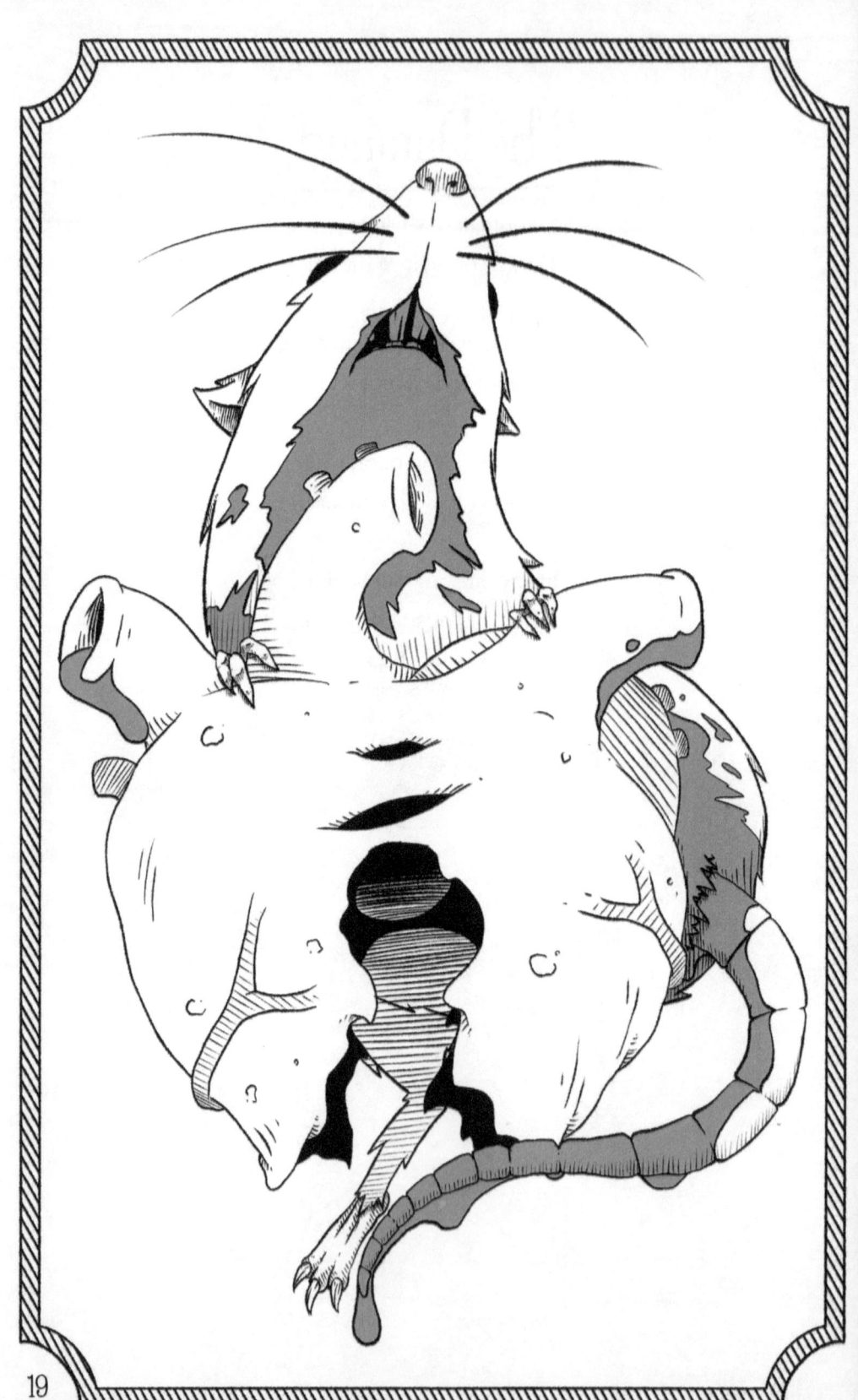

Without End

Today the molten rock will pour
Upon me like the day before.
I wish my flesh to burn no more.
Now, the molten rock, they pour.

From my body skin will tear
Until my blood and bone lay bare.
It seems a waste to say a prayer
When everyday, my skin, they tear.

The rats, each day, eat me alive.
Inside me they will chew and thrive.
And when I die, I'll just revive.
Then rats, again, eat me alive.

Today they'll come and break my heart.
They'll fill it up with love to start,
Then they'll tear the thing apart.
The worst is when they break my heart.

This Old House

This house is alive with something unknown.
It's felt in a shiver, a whisper, a moan.
And since I have lived here it's presence has grown.
Yet only through glances and shadows it's shown.

I've built a contraption that, if I am right,
Will bring from the darkness and into the light -
What lives in the veil now hidden from sight -
that which has haunted me night after night.

I am sad to relay it has worked as expected.
My machine has revealed that this house is infected.
by spirits to whom I am, daily, subjected.
My presence to them seems to go undetected.

Each day a new horror now waits for me here.
In the place I had once called a home and held dear.
I pray that these terrible things disappear.
For each room I enter finds nothing but fear.

Today I will try to fix my machine.
If I can do it then what this would mean
Is an end to the horrible things I have seen.
I will write once again when this old house is clean.

Something Ate Me

Something ate me.
I'm not dead.
There's hardly room here for my head.

It smells in here.
It's fairly damp.
It's also dark and there's no lamp.

The walls are moving.
The air is thick.
Someone help me out here quick!

Whatever ate me
Isn't nice.
At least it cannot eat me twice.

24

Small Town

Where did it come from? Well, nobody knows,
But down in the dark and the silence it grows.

It watches and whispers. It hungers and stares.
We've got to do something, but nobody dares.

The slowly and silent and over the years,
Occasionally somebody just disappears.

We know they were taken, devoured and dead,
But these sorts of things seem to just go unsaid.

We're a happy and prosperous, terrified town.
You can join us, just don't you go poking around.

Sirens Three

The first was a girl with shadows for hair.
She walked into town and stopped in the square.
She sang out her song of fear and despair.
Shriveling up every heart.

The second was fire, she came after fear.
Her song, it brought hate for all that could hear.
Her violent tune drew blood from each ear.
Peace would become a lost art.

The end sang her song, though nobody knew.
A terrible melody none could undo.
Sung out in silence, pitch perfect, on cue.
It tore the whole world apart.

Self Reflection

I really don't care for the mirrors.
That's where the other me lives.
With smiling eyes
And his horrible lies
And the guilt and the grief that he gives.

I try to stay clear of the mirror.
Where the other me watches and waits.
With his dark, empty grin,
Knowing all of my sin,
And those beckoning fiery gates.

Streetlights

As the cold wind whips,
Drawing steam from my lips,
And the moon takes it's cover in clouds,
Creeps the stench and the smile
Of the wretch and the vile
Crawling out from their veils and shrouds.
Every evil of sort
Slowly twists and contorts,
Snatching innocence up in the streets.
So, when your parents say
That it's too dark to play,
Run inside and hide under your streets.

30

Poor Hollow Mary

There's a hole in the chest of a girl named Mary.
That's dark, cold, and endless; her burden to carry.
Inside of the hole lives a horrible thing.
That is hungry and violent and scary.

The monster inside her consumes without end.
On anything living. On stranger or friend.
It swallows their souls until they dry,
Then into the hole they descend.

The hole's getting bigger with each awful deed.
And Mary is scared of its undying need.
The gnawing of hunger is driving her mad.
So, she let's the thing out just to feed.

It won't be too long before Mary is swallowed.
Taken to where the misfortunate wallowed.
Into the hole, poor Mary will go;
Eaten and empty and hallowed.

Precious Cargo

I rarely smile, but when I do,
Know that it's because of you.
Because of you and where you are;
Sweetly sleeping in my car.

More specifically my trunk.
Now, to my house we go...Ka-Thunk!

Pet Rock

I found a rock. A rock from space.
It landed rather near my place.
I picked it up and fell in love.
A feeling I could not replace.

I kept it close. Not close enough.
Getting closer would be tough.
I put the rock inside my mouth.
Swallowing the rock was rough.

I my stomach safe and sound.
There the rock would not be found.
Begging me to feed it meat.
As it starts to move around.

I ate a dog, and then a deer.
Both of which filled me with fear.
Let's not forget about the man
Who's begging I will always hear.

Then from my stomach, out it burst,
With smaller rocks that it had nursed.
With slimy limbs they crawled away.
The loss I felt was just the worst.

Paint

Red in the bathroom, the kitchen, the hall.
A hypnotic color; I must paint it all.
A beautiful color; so full of life.
That sweet kind of red that you get with a knife.

But, oh, how I'm troubled! I paint night and day.
For when the paint dries, the red fades away.
I guess I'll keep painting, 'till all of it's red.
I'll gather more paint 'til the day I am dead.

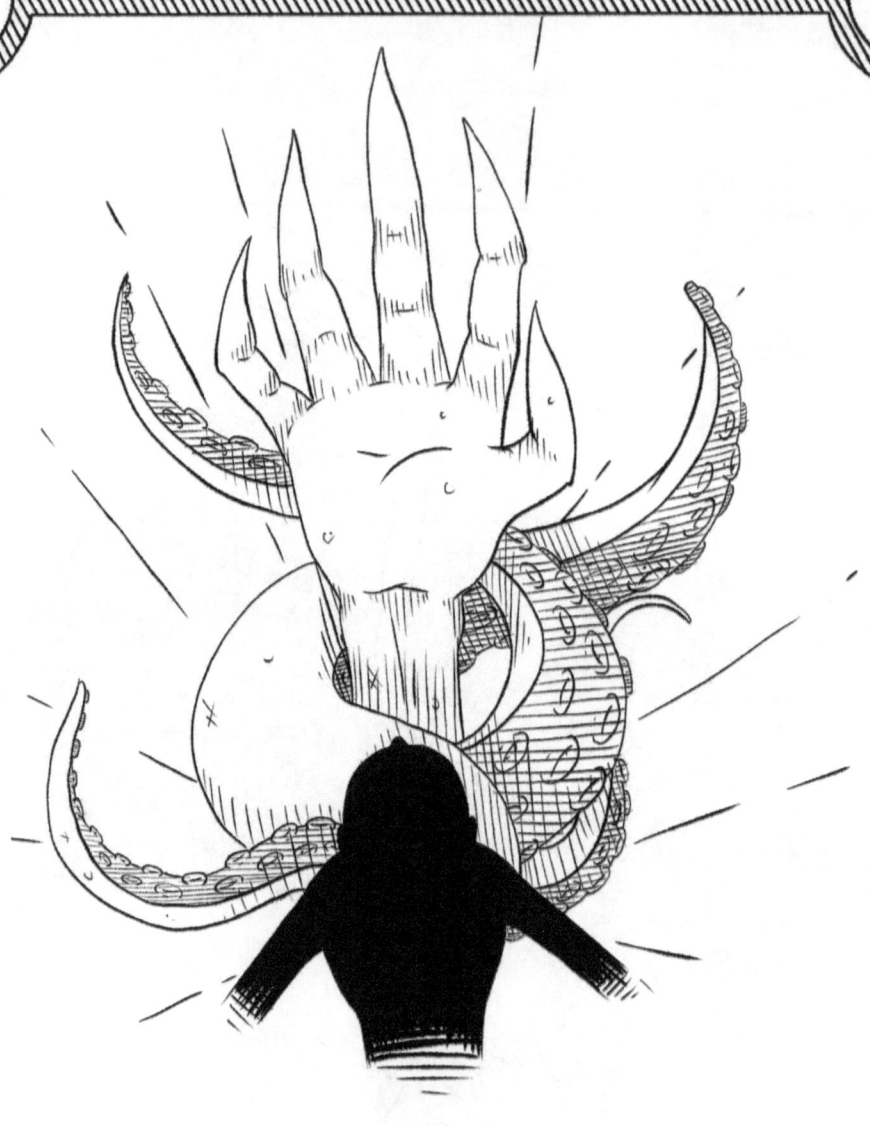

Other Worldly

What we have done we may never undo.
Inscriptions were written and words spoken, too.
The portal is open, and evil pours through.
This flesh, now a doorway, will make the world new.

Old Severed Head

When I woke, in the night, at the end of my bead
Watching me sleep was an old severed head.

It spoke with a quiet and crackly voice,
"Listen up good. I will give you a choice."

"Your body of soul, which one will be mine?"
"Take my soul," I said frightened, "I don't need it. It's fine."

The head, it then smiled and started to scream.
I cackled and roared like a horrible dream.

Then the blood and the bone poured out of the head.
Then the muscle and skin took a shape on my bed.

Now, standing before me, this naked mad man,
Grabbed onto my head with both of his hands.

Then gave it a squeeze and a bit of a twist.
He yanked my head off with a flick of his wrist.

Then he took me and dropped me on some stranger's bed.
Who awoke to the sight of an old severed head.

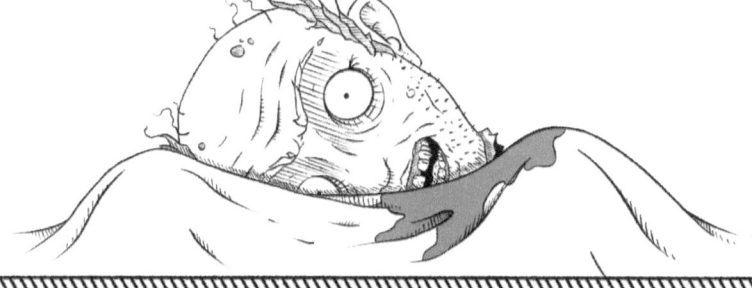

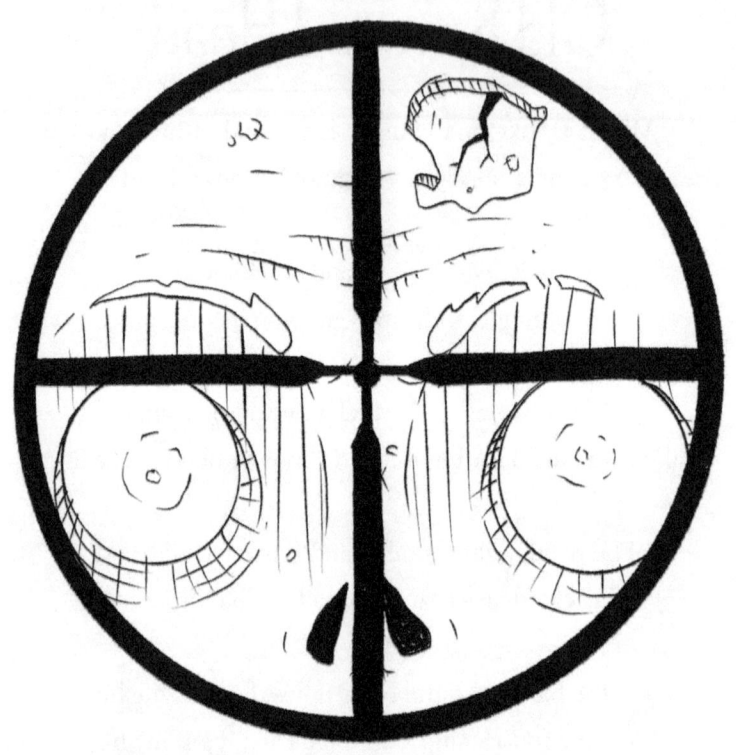

One Down

On the roof with my scope,
My little glass eye.
All alone through my scope,
The zombies and I.

Through the lens of my scope,
we stand face to face.
To them, just my bullet
Ever feels out of place.

Murder Bot

I built myself a murder bot.
It likes to murder quite a lot.

One problem I did not foresee -
Is that it's try to murder me.

If you see my murder bot -
It may kill you, it may not.

I just thought that you should know.
If it's coming, you should go.

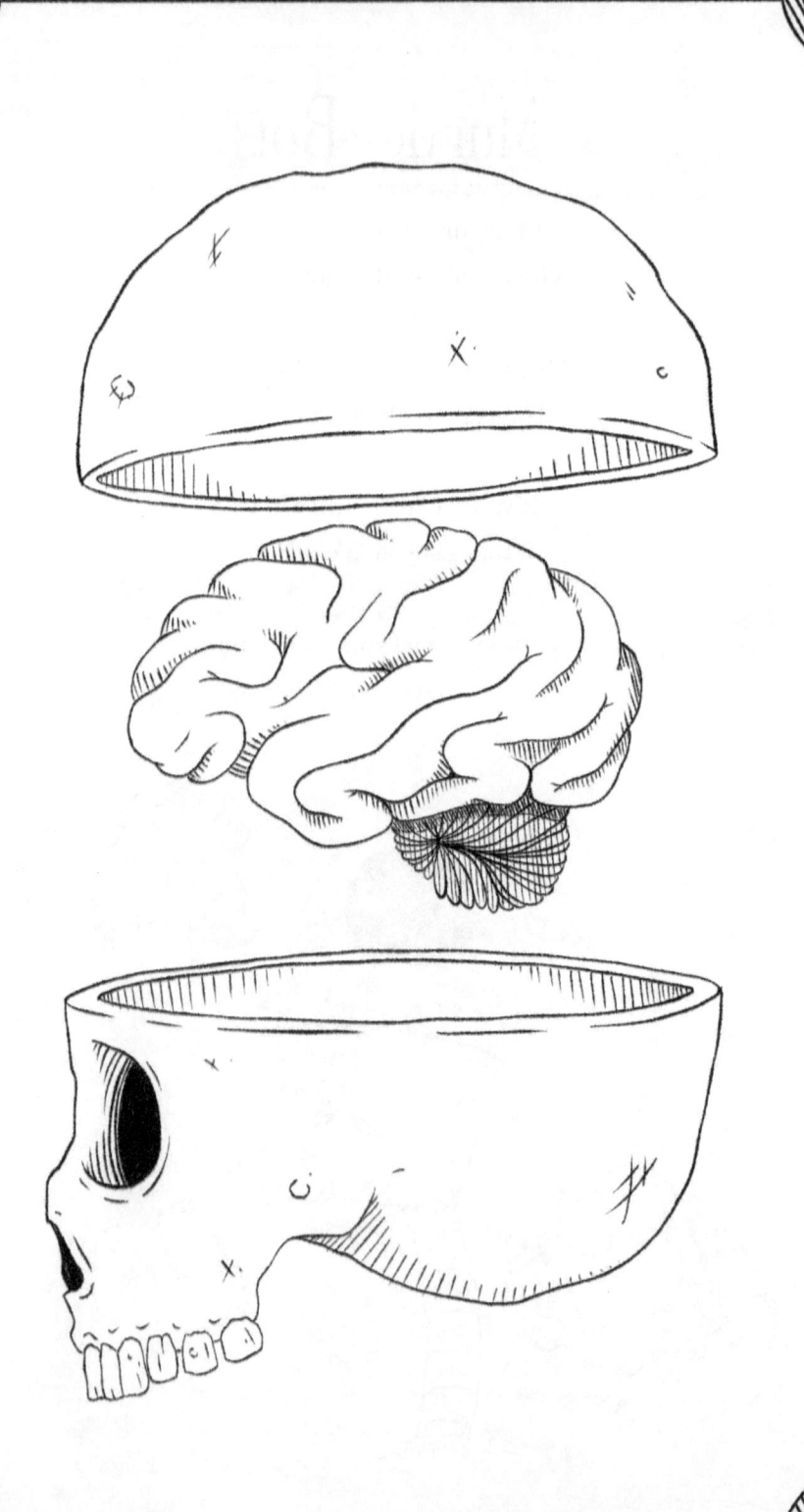

Meatball

I'm a wrinkled ball of meat.
Trapped inside a box of bone.
In a clumsy suit of flesh.
In a lovely wooden home.
On a tiny spinning rock.
In an endless, empty space.
I'm a wrinkled ball of meat.
Come and gone without a trace.

Little Whispers

Deep inside my head there lives a voice I've never seen.
Of cunning mind, clever word, and temperament so mean.

It hides away, deep in my mind, and rarely tries to fight.
But it's words slink and make me think of things I find a blight.

I'm told it's only in my mind, but I can feel it squirm.
Some kind of tiny creature. Perhaps and evil worm?

Oh, yes! Of course! A worm, a worm! Not much else it could be.
Oh no, they'll think I'm crazy...

BUT SOON WE'LL MAKE THEM SEE!

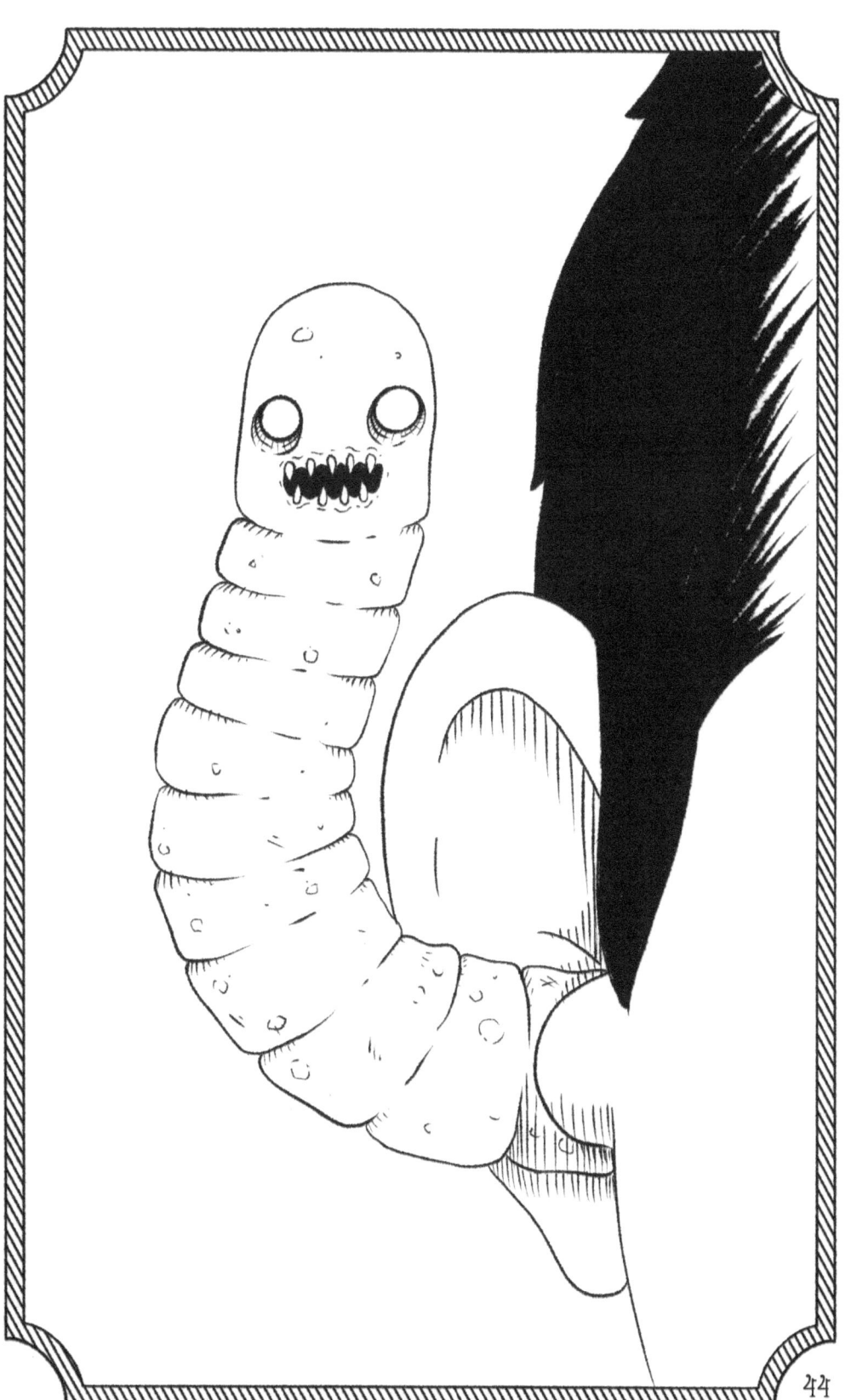

Moonlit Dreams

Dreams, I know, are never real.
But, oh, the fear they make me feel.

Dreams of panic; frenzied chase.
I wish I couldn't keep their pace.

But in my dreams I'm much too quick,
And those I chase just look so sick.

Flush with fright and disbelief,
And all I give is violent grief.

Then blood and bones and gnashing teeth.
Full moon above and I beneath.

These dreams, I know, are never real.
But fear, and full, they make me feel.

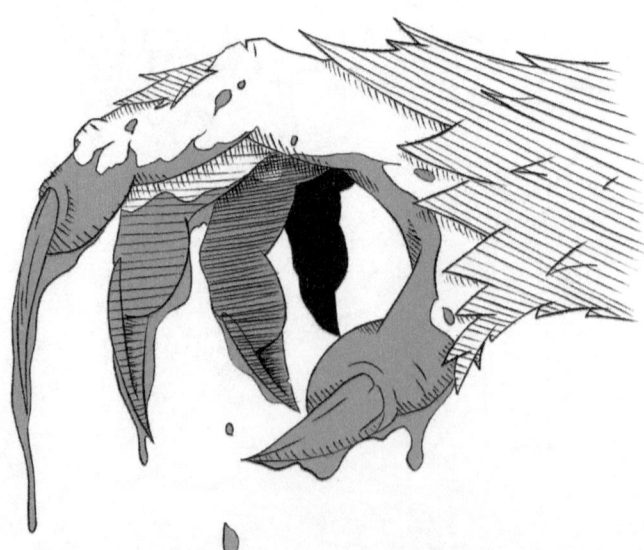

This Box

Last night I had a funny dream.
It was a bit bizarre.
I was walking down the street
And got hit by a car.

Death came by and took my hand.
He told me not to fear.
My funeral was beautiful.
Death even shed a tear.

Afterwards, Death guided me
Into a shining light.
And at that moment everything
Felt like it was right.

Then I woke up from that dream -
In the dark where I survive -
'Cause someone made a huge mistake
And buried me alive.

My Friends

Skeletons, my only friends,
I see them dance about.
Stuck inside their fleshy cages
Wanting to get out.

Worry not, my bony friends,
For I have found the key!
I'll simply rip you out of there
So you can be with me.

Mr. Long Bones

Mr. Long Bones used to live next door
'Til the day he died, now he don't no more.
And even though he is long since dead,
I can see him still when I go to bed.

Out my window and on his roof,
And though I haven't a shred of proof,
In the dead of night I can always see
Mr. Long Bones coming right toward me.

Of Nightmares

At night I hide with extra care.
The nightmares come from everywhere.
I dare not blink for fear of sleep.
The nightmares find me there.

When I wake, first thing I see
Is sunshine mocking bright with glee.
The nightmares come, and too they pass,
But take a piece of me.

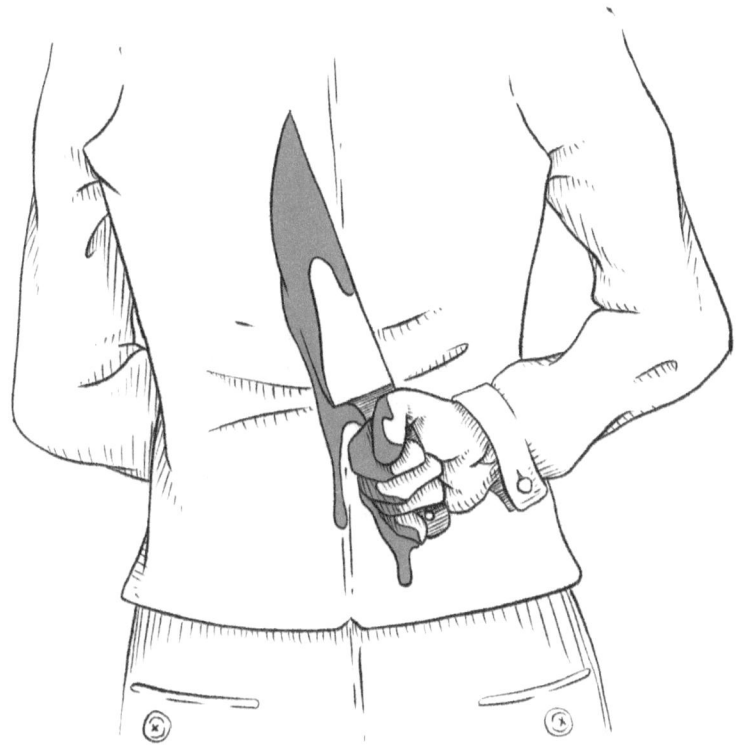

One Who Butles

"A murder in the powder room!"
"It's the butler," they assume.
I'd like to scream about such things,
But I'm at work so I'll abstain.

I'll carry on with dignity
While, one by one, they point at me.
I'd shake my bloodied glove, "For shame!"
But, perhaps, I am to blame.

Madam Shirin

He met her inside of a small hidden shop
That he found on a whim when he paused for a stop.
The sign on the door it read, "Fortunes inside"
And the door gave a chime when he opened it wide.

She beckoned him over and into a chair,
Then held out her hand and flipped back her hair.
"Ten dollars is all I will need to begin."
So he paid and he listened to Madam Shirin.

Her voice was like honey poured over his ear
But the fortune she told him brought nothing but fear.
His life would end soon and Shirin told him when.
Death would come visit at a quarter to ten.

He didn't believe it but then saw her eyes
Welled up full of tears to the young man's surprise.
"I'm sorry," she told him, "But this is your fate."
So he gave her a kiss before it was too late.

Then took off out the shop and back to his place
Where he worried and plotted and, back and forth, paced.
But all he could think of was Madam Shirin
And then inspiration had struck from within.

At a quarter to ten, when Death had come by,
A note on the door had caused Death to sigh.
"Dear Death," it was written," I'm sorry, I'm out."
"Please stop by another time when you're about."

Death crumpled the note and tossed it in the bin.
How was this possible? Where to begin?
So Death turned around and went on his way,
And made his own note to come back the next day.

Each day the man went back to Madam Shirin.
She'd tell him his fortune so Death could not win.
And before not too long the man captured her heart.
So they married and never again would they part.

The years soon went by and like each one before.
The man would leave notes, just for Death, on the door.
The man would then leave before Death would arrive.
So that he and Shirin could, together, survive.

One day though Death came when the old man was out.

And again was the note for which Death had no doubt.

But he opened the door and he let himself in.

For today he had come too for Madam Shirin.

Death came the next day to the old weeping man.

"Can you tell me," Death asked, "Was this part of your plan?"

So the man said to Death, "Okay then, let's go."

"All my love has been taken. I've nothing but woe."

But Death turned his back with one last thing to say.

"Well you wanted to cheat me, so living you'll stay."

And the man is still weeping 'till this very day.

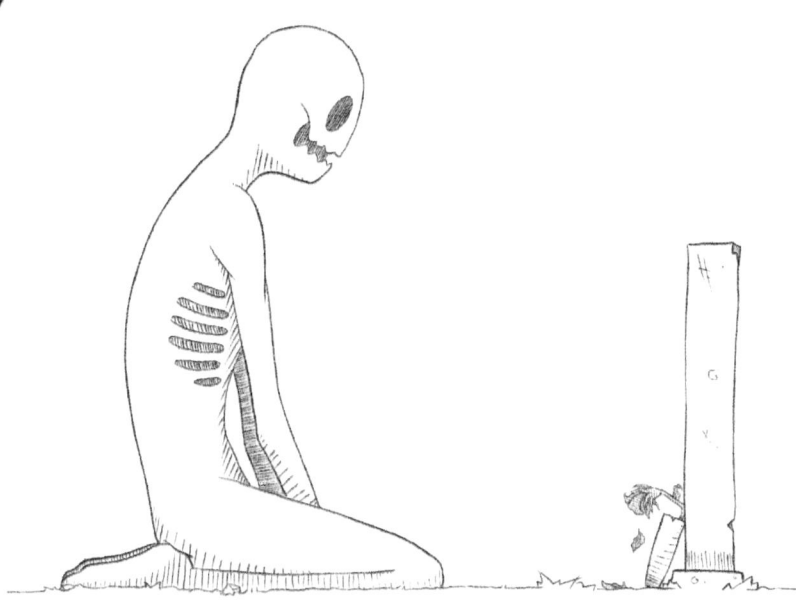

Regret

I've never been so silent.
I've never been so still.
I've never been so all alone.
I never had the will.

I've never been so broken.
I've never been so scared.
I never thought about the end.
I never really cared.

I always knew how hard it was,
Not how bad it could get.
I knew how much it hurt to live,
But now I know regret.

Timmy's Tummy

Little Timmy's tummy hurt.
Perhaps because he ate some dirt.

For in that dirt there crawled a bug,
That now, inside of Timmy, dug.

A scary fact he never knew.
Inside of him it grew and grew.

One night, while he was fast asleep,
Out of his tummy did it creep.

It split his tummy right in two!
Oh no, what would his mother do?

She'd grab a knife and then attack
And fight to get her Timmy back.

But Timmy lay there, soaked in red,
Split in two upon his bed.

His mother sat beside and said,
"Sleep soundly dear. That bug is dead."

What's for Dinner?

Mr. Smith complained quite a lot.
Most recent? "The water's too hot!"
Mrs. Smith replied, "Good!"
"Then it's just as it should!"
Then she put the lid back on the pot.

Souls Here

Souls! Souls! Come get your Souls!
Dripping with sin and tasty on rolls!
Dip them in fire or eat them from bowls!
What are you waiting for? Come get your souls!

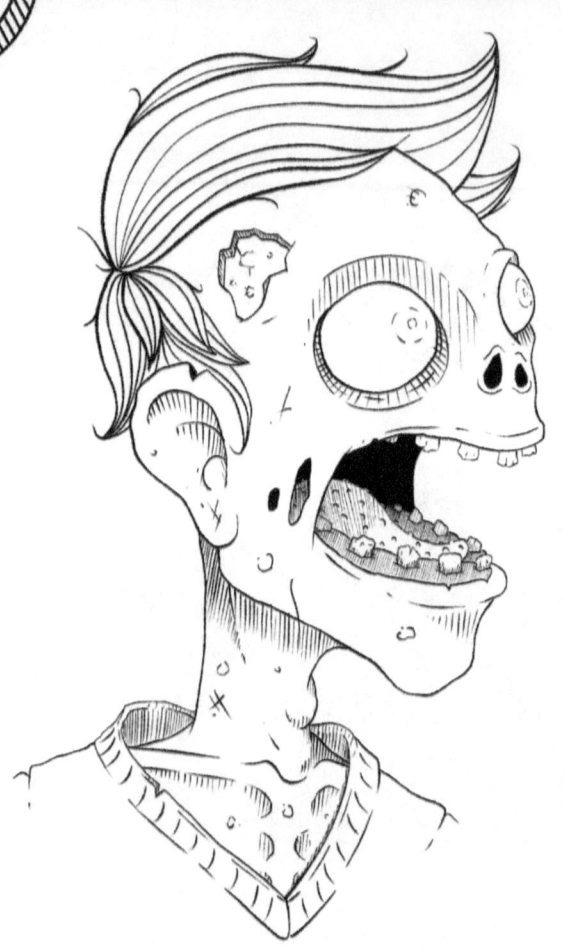

Zombie Town

There once was a young boy, unlike the rest.
Who acted alive, oh he tried his best.
He looked kinda different, skin turning green,
A sad walking corpse that made people scream.

"Kill it with fire!" they'd argue and fight,
"A shot to the brain! That'd put him down right!"
The poor zombie boy preferred not to make scenes.
He'd rather sit silent than suffer their screams.

So off to the woods he'd wander alone
Where animals fled at the sound of his moan.
He'd look for a spot, by himself, he could hide
Where he'd wait for the panic in town to subside.

Today, it so happened, he found a nice stream
And he sat on a rock in a lowly sunbeam.
In the water he let his feet dangle and sway
And he laid himself back and wasted the day.

And the day after that, soon a month had gone by.
As he lay there he thought, "If alive I would cry."
Just then he heard screams and he sat himself up.
Explosions and gunshots from town did erupt.

He hopped to his feet and promptly fell down.
He looked at his legs as he lay on the ground.
"Just perfect", he thought as he lie in dismay,
"That stream has eroded both my feet away!"

He clawed at the dirt and crawled into town
"I've got to find out what the heck's going down!"
And what he found there was a pleasant surprise.
A town full of zombies filled up his dead eyes.

How did this happen? He just didn't know
but he smiled and heard people shouting, "Just go!"
"The water! It's tainted! Just give me your gun!"
"I'll hold'em off! Now hurry up! RUN!"

"My feet in the river", he thought with a grin.
They'd made a whole town full of zombies for him.

Until Forever

My lover, woeful, waits for me
With worry in her eyes.
And by her side I, woeful, haunt
Until the day she dies.

What's in the Box?

What's in the box?

Well pay you no mind.

It's not very pretty.

It's not very kind.

This box is a prison.

A thing to keep locked.

Leave, always, this evil confined.

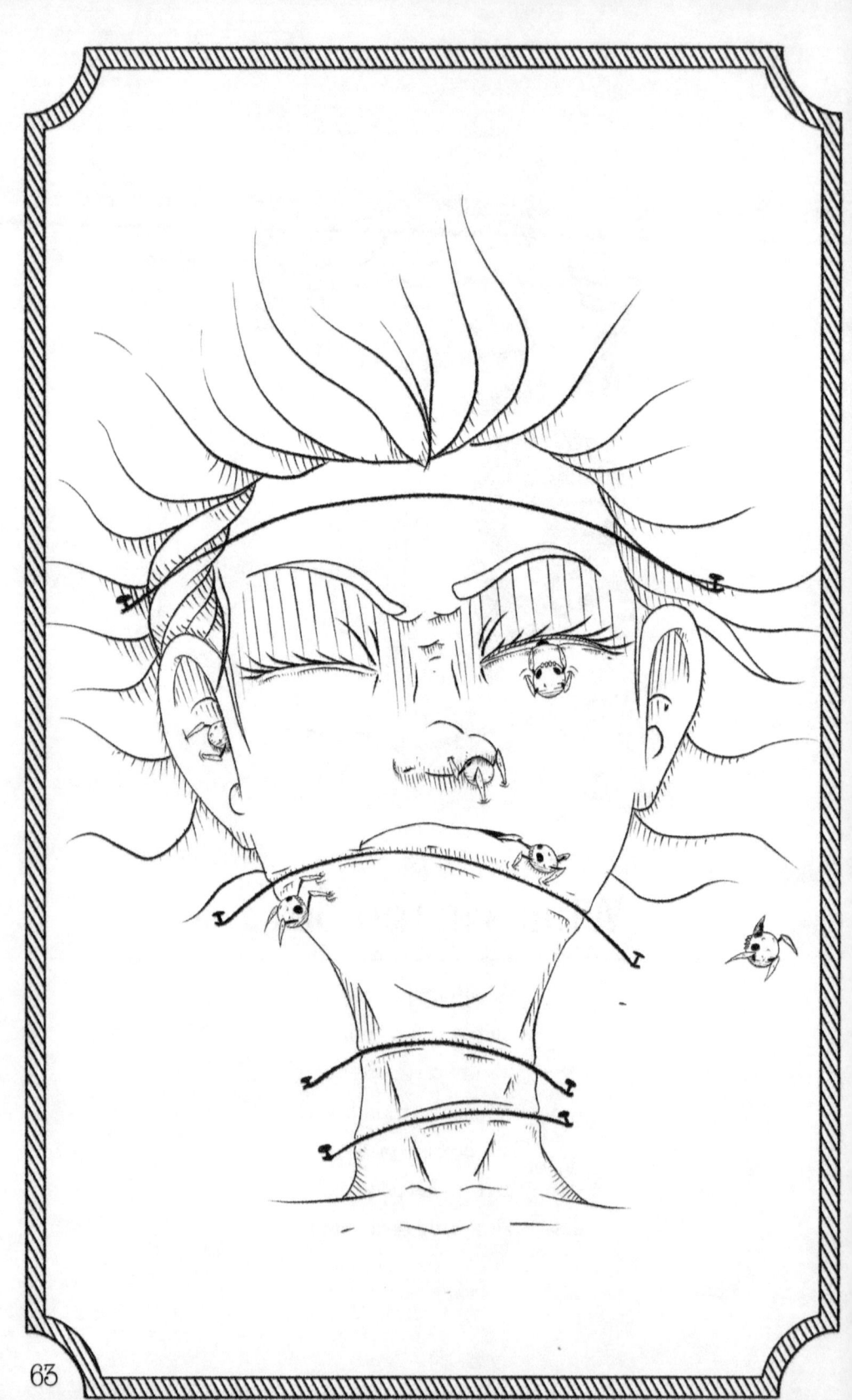

The Little Things

It's the little things in life that find you
When you least expect.
The little things that pop up places
Where you never checked.
The little things will find you
Any place you try to hide
The little things will get you
Once they find their way inside.
The little things are awful
And as viscous as can be
The little things will kill you
If you ever set them free.

My Head is on Fire

My head is on fire!
The consequence dire!
Don't stop to admire!
Get help!

I've burnt to the end.
Where were you my friend?
No help you could send?
Oh welp.

Lockdown

This lab is on lockdown,
So everyone's staying.

There are rules and procedures
In need of obeying.

Containment's been breached,
Much to our dismaying.

This lab is on lockdown.
There's no use in praying.

Good vs Evil

Wear a mask to a ball; you're a dashing young man.
Wear a mask in the woods; they run if they can.

Saw a woman in half in a box; it's a trick.
Saw a woman in half in your cabin; you're sick.

Hang out with your friends at the mall; What a day!
Hang up all your friends on your wall; NOT OKAY!

The world's just something I don't understand.
They act like my being this evil was planned.

The Man in the Mask

Beneath the floor where the angels fell.
Where the wretches weep and the tortured yell.
Where the fire cleans and the horrors dwell.
Comes slithering up from a bubbling well.

A terrible thing, time long and forgot.
Eyes full of fire and a heart full of rot.
Words made of sickness and blistering hot.
Familiar with mercy; he's certainly not.

He'll toy with your mind and leech off your soul.
He'll tell a lie you'll gobble up whole.
He'll twist you and turn your heart darker than coal.
Then watch as you waste in a bottomless hole.

He looks like a man but his flesh is a mask.
To bring suffering is his singular task.
None know his true form and I wouldn't dare ask.
Beware of this man. The man in the mask.

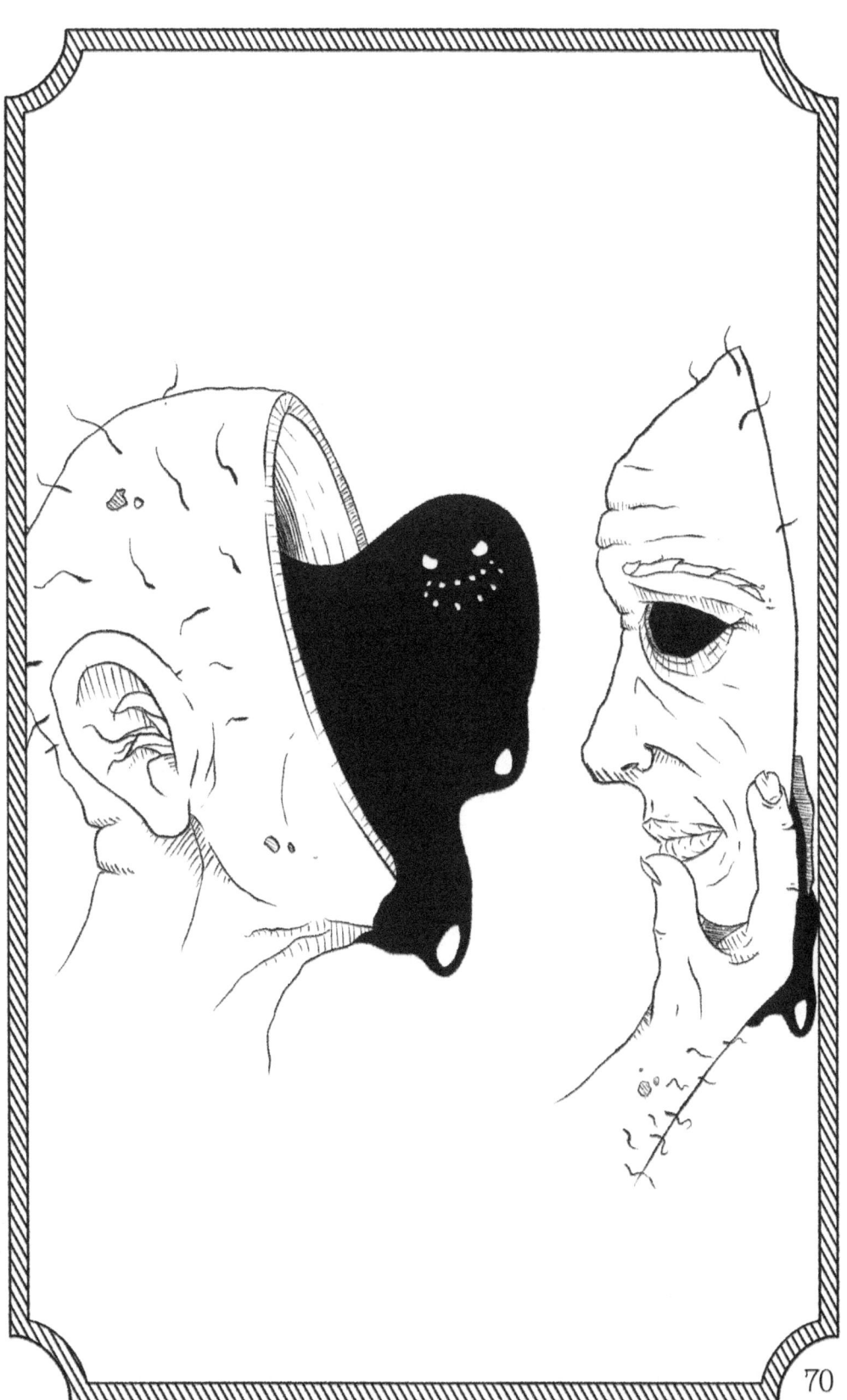

Reaching Out

A loss is like drowning, the world you knew,
Is distant and muffled and rather askew.

The longer you're down there the more that it hurts.
As your last bit of hope bubbles out now in spurts.

As loved ones reach under to grab for your hand.
To pull you up, drag you back, on to dry land.

But the bottom seems closer and easy to choose.
It is quiet and empty with nothing to lose.

But what would your loved one say now if they knew.
If they saw you had given up; what would they do?

They'd tell you they love you. That they understand.
Then beg you to reach out and grab someone's hand.

Shifting Sands

On ancient shores of bloody sands
An obelisk before me stands.
Old and stone and dripping red,
It bleeds on shores now long and dead.
Words are carved into the stone.
Words that should be left alone.
But yet I march and out I reach.
I wade through death upon the beach.
I touch the stone and read aloud.
As duty bound I'm rather proud.
I give into the obelisk.
Denying it would run the risk
That creatures underneath the sand
Would rise and overrun the land.

Having a Ball

I got a bunch of people. It wasn't hard at all.
More difficult was stitching all of them into a ball.

The ones inside are dead now. On that I'd surely bet.
The ones outside are simply the ones who have not died yet.

The ones on top are lucky, just gazing at the sky.
The ones upon the sides just sit and watch the world go by.

The ones along the bottom, they have it worst of all.
Stuck carrying the burden for the rest upon the ball.

Big Storm

The clouds are rolling in once more,
But not the kinds that rain and pour,
The kinds with legs of giant beasts
That stomp and smash and roar.

Incomplete

The incomplete are everywhere.
So, if you've got a part to spare
They'll take from you. They do not care.
The incomplete are everywhere.

The incomplete will come for you.
They'll maybe take an ear or two.
You'll feel less than when they're through.
The incomplete will come for you.

The incomplete are never done.
They take a piece of anyone.
You cannot hide, you cannot run.
The incomplete are never done.

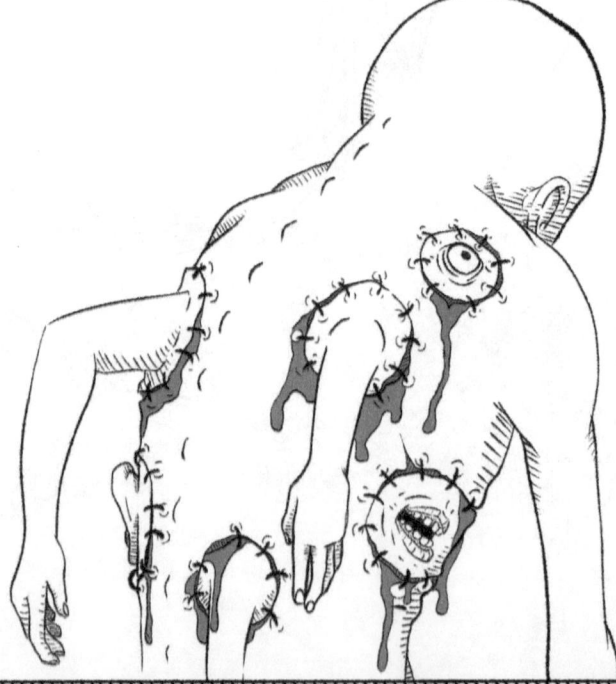

Bedtime Buddies

From beneath Billy's bed
Came a something that said
"Dear boy I could sure use a friend."

Young Billy replied
With his eyes very wide,
"Are you real or are you pretend?"

"Oh now don't be silly."
"Of course I'm real Billy."
"And quite lonely. On that you can bet."

"Now if you would please."
"I need something to squeeze."
"Perhaps you could bring me a pet?"

So Billy grabbed Rover
And brought him right over
And slid him right under the bed.

And then, suddenly
All Billy could see
Was a splattering puddle of red.

"Is that blood?" Billy cried
"Has my poor Rover died?"
It replied, "Don't be silly my boy."

"It's not blood that you see."
"Rover's happy with me."
"Oh no those are just my tears of joy."

"Well that's a relief."
"I was stricken with grief."
"Can I come in and play with you too?"

"Soon enough son"
"But we are not done"
"I've got one more thing for you to do."

"I've been so alone."
"No family of my own."
"A new mommy and dad would be swell."

Billy thought for a while
Then spoke with a smile
"I guess I can bring them as well."

"That would bring me great joy!"
Something said to the boy
As Billy ran right out the room.

Then something just waited.
It hungrily waited.
For the family that it would consume.

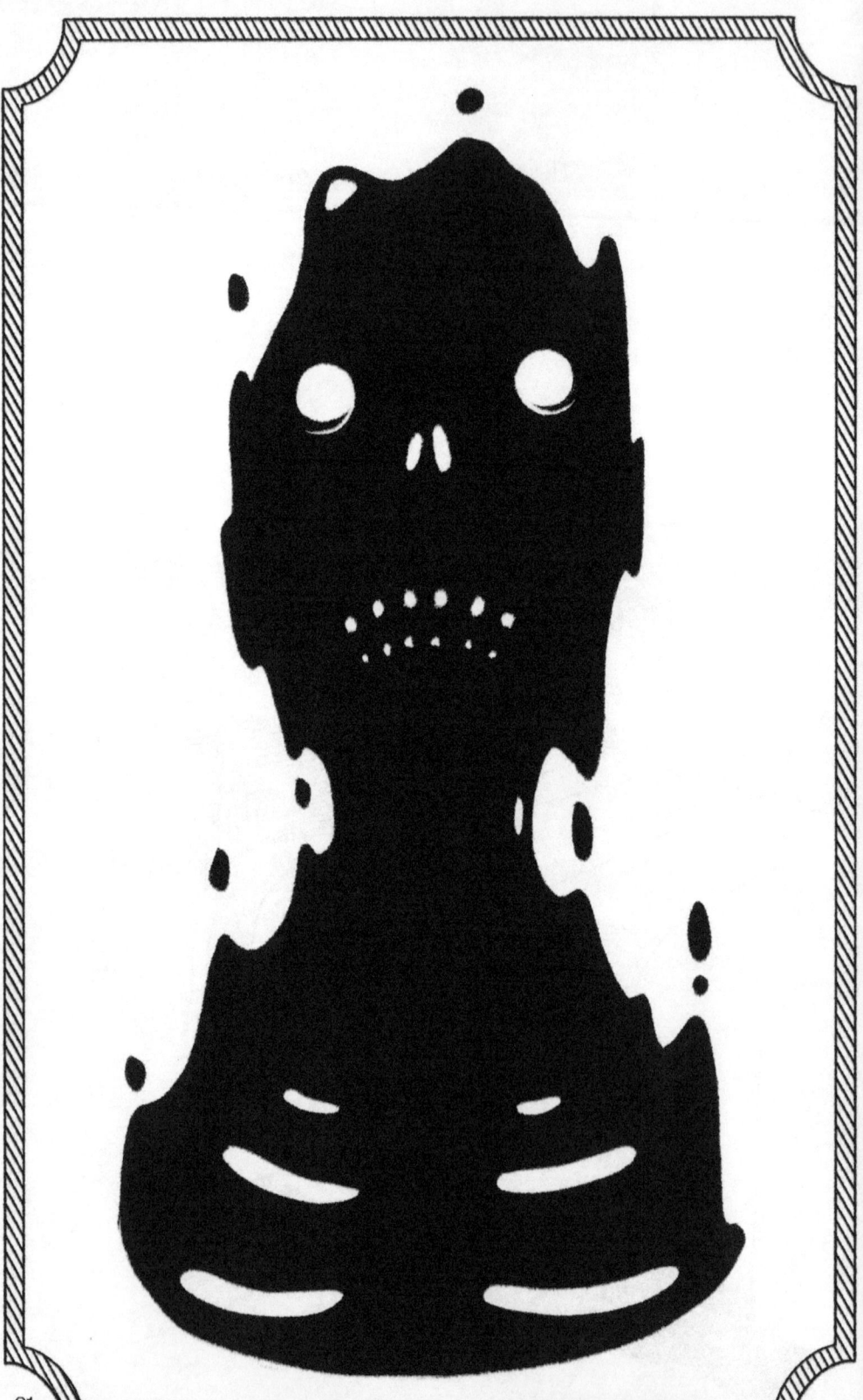

Goodnight Kiss

A dark silhouette,
One whom I'd never met,
Telling me this has all been a dream.

As I lay in my bed,
Struck immobile with dread,
Flowing tears down my face in a stream.

She inches her way
Through the absence of day,
As I draw upon shallowing breath.

She purses her lips,
And touches their tips
On my cheek with her cold kiss of death.

Blood Beasts

Don't linger in mists where the blood beast are found.
They have do not have eyes and can't hear a sound.
They know where you are. There is nowhere to hide.
They can smell all the blood you've got pumping inside.

Cold Fish

A trip to the fair.
A game for a buck.
A ring on a bottle.
A rare spot of luck.

The prize I had won -
A shimmering gold -
That wouldn't eat much
Except body parts cold.

Creepy Crawlies

Creepy Crawlies in my wall.
I hear them scratch and scrape and crawl.
I dare not sleep a wink at all
With creepy crawlies in my wall.

Creepy Crawlies in my bed.
The thought of sleep fills me with dread.
I dare not rest my weary head
with creepy crawlies in my bed.

Creepy Crawlies in my pants.
They make me squirm and itch and dance.
I fear I do not stand a chance
With creepy crawlies in my pants.

Creepy Crawlies in my ear,
They fill me with such awful fear,
The only things that I can hear
are creepy crawlies in my ear.

Creepy crawlies in my brain
Slowly driving me insane.
All I feel now is pain,
With creepy crawlies in my brain.

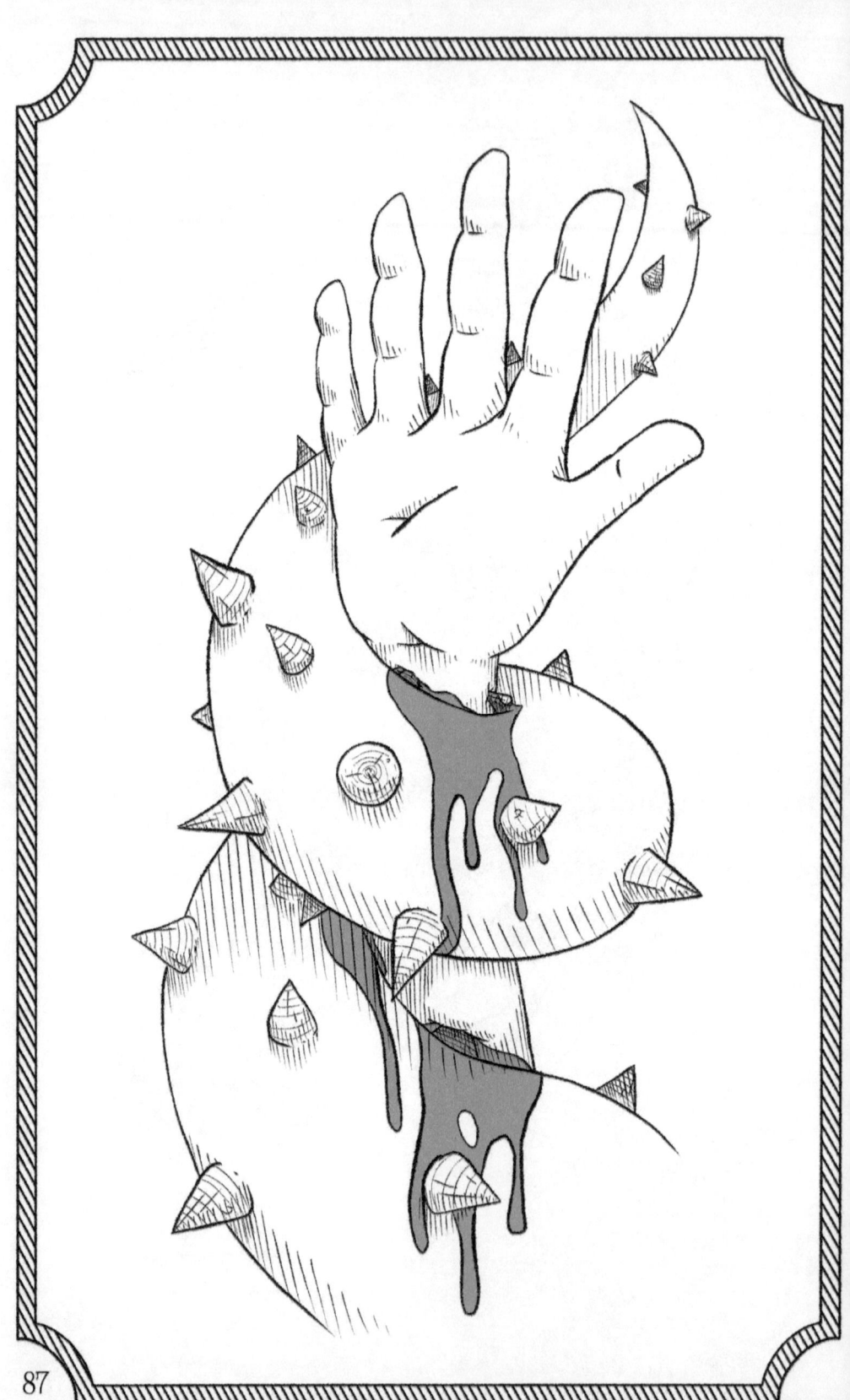

Spring has Sprung

Fall was filled with rotting leaves and anger chilled the air.
A child had gone missing and townsfolk knew not where.
It also happened that a stranger came to town that day.
And though she'd only got there, upon her the blame they'd lay.

They marched her just outside of town, before the firing squad.
And there, blind folded, down she fell into the blood soaked sod.
And there she'd rot as winter came and buried her in white.
While folks in town forgot her and slept safe and warm at night.

And as the winter wandered through it's snowy covered trees.
Just outside town the woman's spirit spread like a disease.
And when the winter thawed away. When spring had come around.
The snowy blanket melted off the long and slumbered ground.

But where the green grass should have been grew vines that dripped with red.
Creeping forth to greet them like the long forgotten dead.
And as the townsfolk gathered to discuss the crimson ground.
From beneath them came an awfully deep and angry sound.

Then from the ground did burst more vines that towered to the sky.
That hung for just a moment then descended from on high.
They wrapped around each living soul in thick and thorny strands.
Then pulled them down and deep beneath their cursed and bloodied lands.

Left Overs

I'll piece them together from what is left over
Of Billy and Suzie and their poor dog Rover.
I told them my lab was no place for their tricks
But what has befallen them now I will fix.

Arise for me Billy and Suzie and Rover
Or at least the new beast made from what was left over.

Little Beasties

I feed the beasties every night.
Cutest little things.
Fuzzy little cuddle muffins,
Even with their fangs.

They're sorta growing kinda quick.
Bigger than I thought.
They always shiver like they're cold,
Though I keep it hot.

Today they all grew little wings;
Hovered to and fro.
Now what exactly are these things?
That I do not know.

My little beasties once were cute,
Something to admire,
But then they started breathing flames;
Set my house on fire.

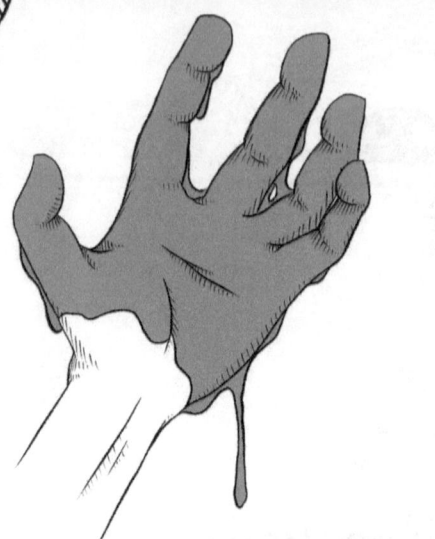
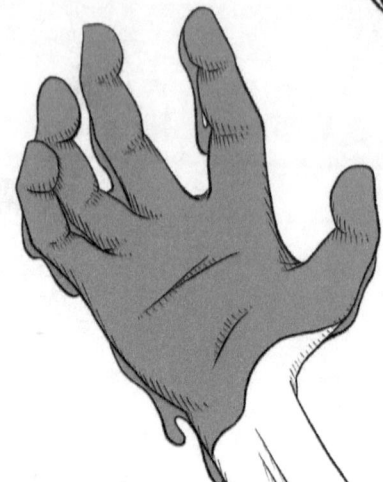

Just a Little Bit More

How much further you ask?
Just a little bit more.
Past the blood on your hands
And the tears on the floor.

Past the screams in the night
And the pain of regret.
Through the lives you have taken
And the ones you've not yet.

Past the terror and madness
You've long since embraced,
And the still to come horrors
You haven't yet faced.

Through the blood and the bile
And the mountains of gore.
I have seen what you've done.
What's a little bit more?

Inconvenience Mart

That gas station burrito was good but not great.
I'm regretting now every bite that I ate.

I've not eaten since. That was two days ago.
Yet the size of my stomach continues to grow.

It's a bubbling, wriggling, mess in my belly.
The gas that I pass from each end is so smelly.

I can feel now something is ripping through me!
Was it something I ate? Wonder what it could be?

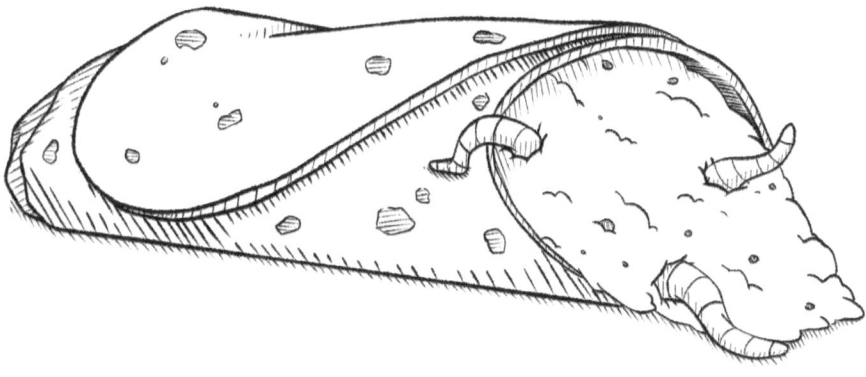

Hole

Yesterday
While on a stroll,
I started falling;
No control.
Hell, it seems,
Has found my soul.
And now I pay
My debts in full.

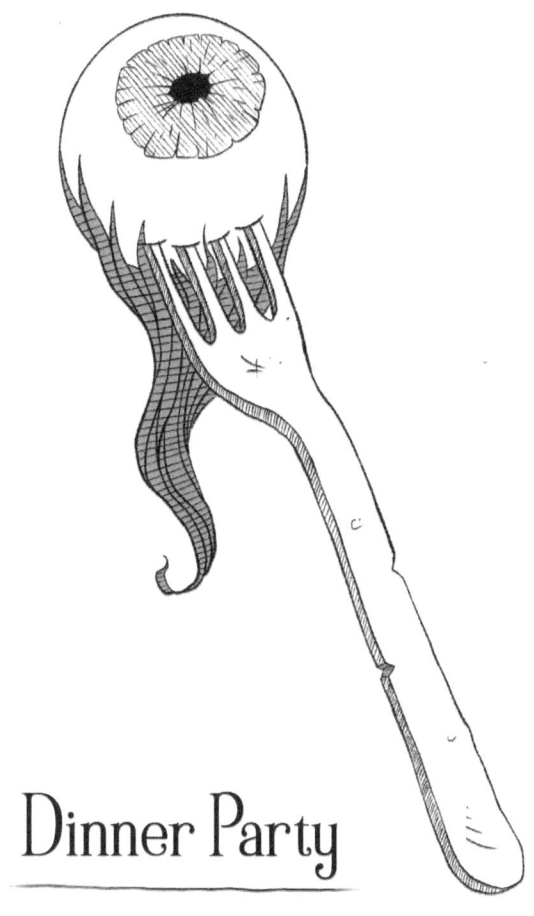

Dinner Party

You tried to leave,

I made you stay,

But in the end you went away.

Your company

Was such a treat,

But better still was all your meat.

Infestation

The fog laden breeze,
The death in the trees,
Where bodies a swing and a sway.

They whisper of sorrows
And stolen tomorrows.
The woven invite you stay.

The skittering sound
Of those underground
Beneath the homes empty and black.

So tread very light,
This town has a blight,
That's lying in wait to attack.

Gimmie Back My Skin

Somebody stole my skin.
Don't believe it? Well it's true.
If I find who stole it
There's no telling what I'll do.
To pain I've grown accustomed,
And it's driving me insane.
If I don't get my skin back.
Everyone will feel my pain.

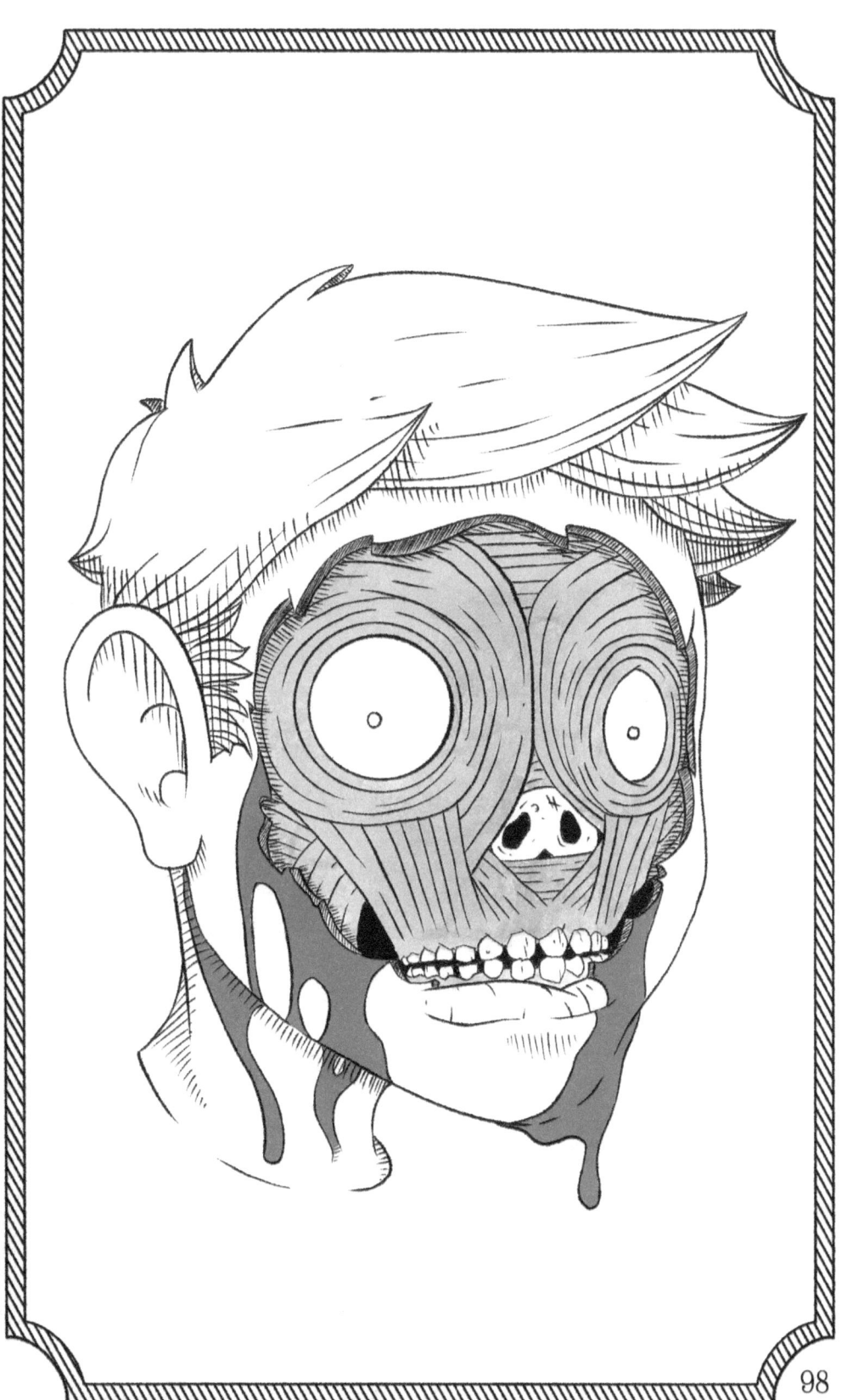

Forever Young

My babies, my babies, why do you keep growing?
As if you have important places you're going.

As if you just wanted your distance from me.
As if you were trapped and you want to be free.

I had you to keep you, forever and ever.
I had you to love you and let you go never.

So you won't be going. No. Babies you'll keep.
With porcelain faces, wide eyed and asleep.

Follow Me

I wouldn't care if you cut me in two.
Start at my head and go all the way through.
'Cause I've got a spirit that's following me,
And I know it won't leave 'til I do.

I wouldn't mind if you cut off my head.
Fed it to zombies 'tween slices of bread.
'Cause I've got a spirit that's following me,
And I know it won't leave 'til I'm dead.

I wouldn't care if you tore out my heart.
Ate it for brunch or turned it to art.
'Cause I've got a spirit that's following me,
And I know it won't leave 'til I part.

I wouldn't mind if you stayed by my side.
You could help me to run, you could help me to hide.
'Cause I've got a spirit that's following me,
And I know it won't leave 'til I've died.

Fair Lady Death

Red were the tears,
Cold was the breath,
Still was the heart
Of the fair lady death.

Black were the wings,
Grey was the hair,
Soft was the kiss
Of my dead lady fair.

Dark Deeds

We do our deeds in the dead of night,
And if you're scared then we've done them right,
And if you're not then we'll do them worse,
'Til you kick and scream and cry and curse.
'Til the fear has gripped you nice and tight,
We'll do our deeds in the dead of night.

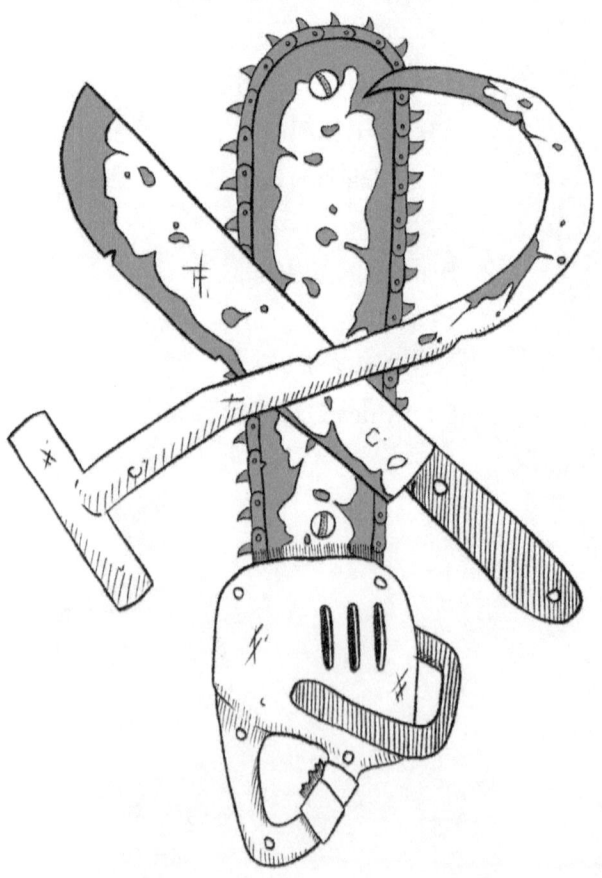

Fallen

I will love you, this I swear,
Though broken dreams with tender care.

And if for you the sun won't shine,
I'll clip my wings to make you mine.

Clowns

Don't worry little fella,
I'm a friendly clown.
Don't you cry,
Now dry your eye,
Why don't you settle down.

Don't worry little buddy,
The circus is around.
Just stay a while,
Crack a smile,
And don't you make a sound.

Don't worry little partner,
Now you will live with me.
Your mom and dad,
They won't be sad,
Because they cease to be.

Don't worry little kiddo,
You'll have a happy life.
And once you're big,
Just like a pig,
I'll carve you with my knife.

Dark Heart

When his dark heart is beating all bloody and black,

The king will awaken to come take it back.

And if the old king and his heart come to bind,

Then this land and darkness shall too be entwined.

A king of the damned, so vicious and cruel.

A kingdom of shadow is what he will rule.

So look but don't touch, and **DO NOT** make a peep.

It is vital the heart of the king stay asleep.

Left Haunted

I see them, they don't see me.

Invisible I am.

A specter of a former life.

They do not understand.

I talk but no one hears me.

I speak to no avail.

Some contact's all I long for,

But every time I fail.

To be with friends and family

Is what I want the most.

I walk around, last man alive,

With nothing but their ghosts.

Behind You

It wants you to look but don't.
It says you'll be fine. You wont.

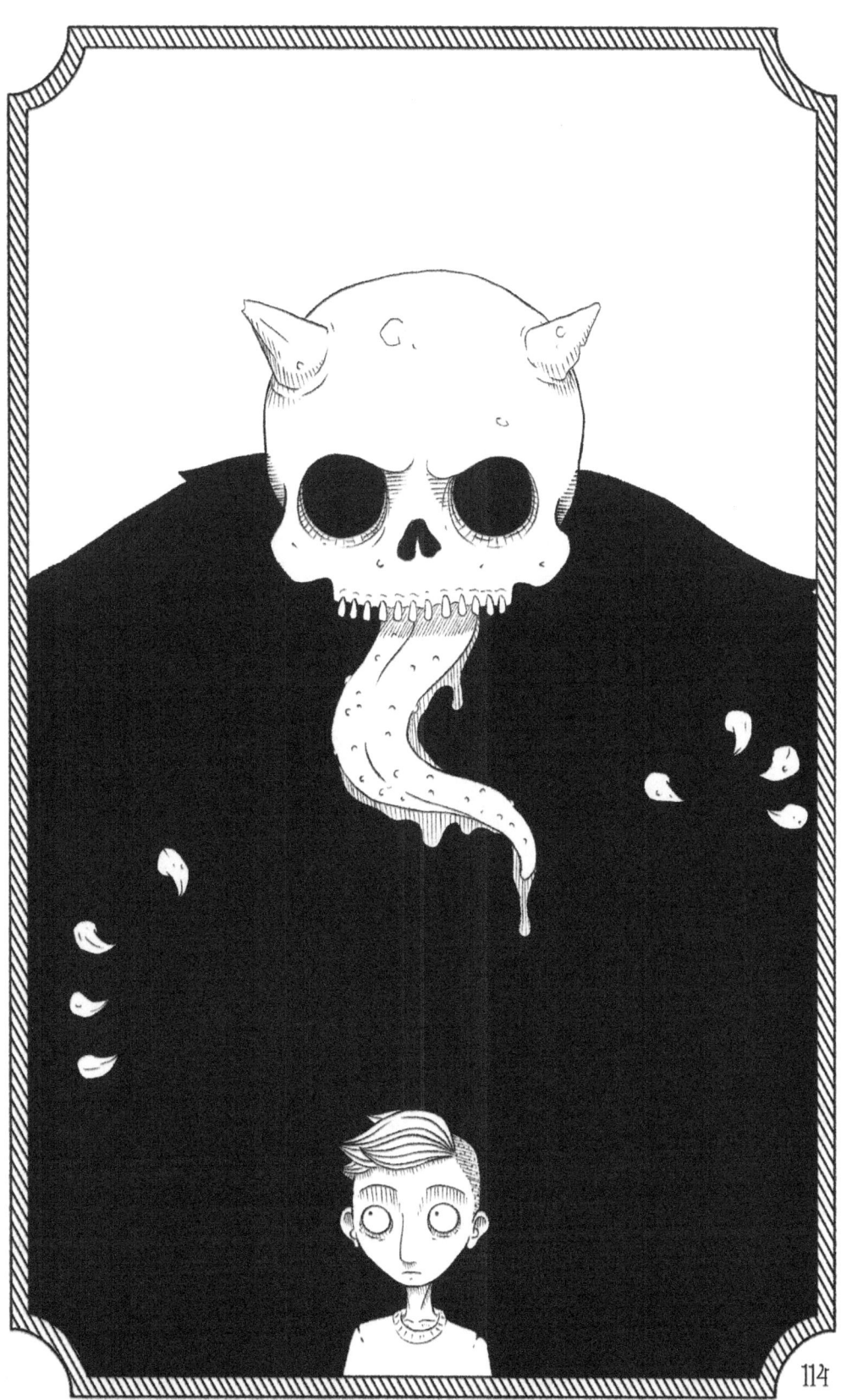

Daddy's Little Girl

Good morning dear!
How are you sweetie?
Time for breakfast.
Something meaty.

Baby girl.
You're so pretty.
Go ahead now
Eat the kitty.

I know you're hungry,
promise baby,
Next I'll bring a person
...maybe.

The Woods

They are waiting in the woods.
They are waiting for a meal.
So I've locked myself inside,
Not knowing who or what is real.

The trees I think are moving,
Or is it just my mind?
They almost got me once
When they snuck from behind.

My dog wasn't so lucky
I miss the little guy
Alone I sit and wait
And watch my life go ticking by.

It's been a few days now
So I think I'll make a run
And if they catch me then they catch me
But at least the waiting's done.

A Void at all Costs

Now, it seems, it's come to this.
Drifting in the cold abyss.
Not knowing if it's moments or if years have passed me by.

To observe it was our mission.
A new, yet very old, transmission
That came to us out of the awfully cold and ancient sky.

Foolish we to not be wary.
And venture interplanetary.
So far from home and out into the empty void we'd fly.

Swiftly though, upon arrival,
Our mission shifted to survival,
As every plan we'd laid before us soon had gone awry.

What was waiting for us there
Was something so beyond compare,
The terror and the beauty was enough to make me cry.

A planet, no, this thing was not.
So unlike anything we'd thought.
A living thing so massive it was hard to quantify.

It looked at us, or rather, in.
Where did we end or it begin?
As now I know not either where I am or even why.

The Last Night

Last night, for fear, from sleep I tore.
Unburied 'neath my heavy snore.
A sound did bound across my floor.
As Death was knocking at my door.

How could I know, well I could tell.
What came with Death; a sickly smell.
I shouted, "Leave! I'm feeling well!"
The sound, from knock to pound, did swell.

A tremble took as I did sway.
I hadn't even strength to pray.
The door began to break away.
The sickly smell now strong decay.

His soothing whispers lifted me.
They washed away my wish to flee.
Then back to sleep he let me be.
And Death, eternal, now I see.

Nothing At All

It is nothing that they fear,

That is drawing ever near,

And it comes from out of nowhere when it does.

So they don't acknowledge nothing,

And, in fact, pretend it's something,

Because nothing means that all this never was.

The Measure of Men

At the edge of the crater, I sit once again.
Mourning the ruins; the measure of men.

What started so simply on paper and pen.
Became an empire that towered 'til when

Greed had them living like thieves in a den.
Then orders were given and fighting began.

Until finally where the old world had been;
Now I sit mourning the measure of men.

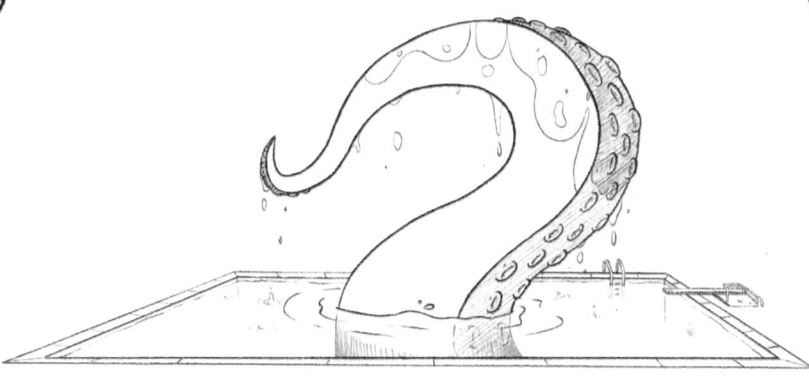

The Depths

At a lovely resort tucked away in the hill.
Where people would come to relax and be still.
Away from the hustle and bustle below.
A place where the wealthy and affluent go.

On a pedestal stood, by the patio door,
A ball made of stone frequent guests would ignore.
It was mostly dark gray, but it sparkled a little,
With an emerald stripe running right through the middle.

And just out the door in the warm summer sun,
Many guests in the pool swam around having fun.
But the patio door caught the eye of a child.
Who saw the round stone, at which the kid smiled.

"Ball," said the child, whose parents ignored.
Who waddled himself to the patio door.
With a mischievous smile he looked all around.
Then reached up for the stone to take it on down.

As he reached for the stone where it stood on its stand.
The boy lost his balance and stone from his hand.
And down the two tumbled, hard, to the floor.
And the stone rolled its way out the patio door.

It rolled past the feet of the guests by the pool.
In the light of the sunset it shone like a jewel.
Then into the water it dropped with a plunk
And down, like the sun on this evening, it sunk.

Then under the water it twisted and turned.
The water glowed green and bubbled and churned.
The guests hurried out. Startled a little.
The stone split in two, down its emerald middle.

The ground gave a rumble and everyone hopped.
The floor of the pool then suddenly dropped.
The guests by the pool looked into the green
That sank into darkness, where nothing was seen.

"Something is down there!" they heard a voice call.
When down in the darkness something did crawl.
Guests all stood watching it, frozen with fear.
As, deep from the depths, the horrors drew near.

One creature then wrapped a large tentacle 'round
A portly old man, lifting him off the ground.
It tightened its grip and it gave him a squeeze,
And popped the large man with an effortless ease.

And then, from the pool, came a terrible sound.
As the blood in the water went splashing around.
The horrible creatures, whipped up in a fury,
Gave chase to the guests who ran off in a hurry.

As one man was running, a young woman tripped.
The man tried to help but then the man slipped.
While falling he dodged some scaly things,
Pouncing at him with its fins spread like wings.

The creatures then struck another instead,
And quickly tore clean the poor victims head.
A couple of others bore into his chest.
Making short work of the unlucky guest.

The woman who'd fallen let out a shrill scream.
But then like some awful and terrible dream,
A huge ragged claw drove right through her throat.
Turning the scream to a gargling note.

The guests ran for cover as night grew chaotic.
They ran and they hid from the horrors aquatic.
And those left alive were all hidden and quiet,
As night settled down from its terrible riot.

The slow and the weak became food by the pool.
As monsters ate hardily dripping in drool.
A housekeeper, "Dani" her name tag had read,
Looked down from above as her heart filled with dread.

Then some guests running by grabbed on to her arm.
Then brought her to hide in their room safe from harm.
They waited the night away quite terrified.
With some of them silent, while some of them cried.

Soon screams filled the halls like a terrible tune,
And Dani knew they would be food rather soon.
Then out of the window, she watched, and she saw
The rock split in two in the gapping green maw.

She decided, right then, she would die either way.
She could do something now or just cower and stay.
So she opened the window and looked at the pool.
From behind her came, "What are you doing, you fool!"

She dove toward the water in one graceful leap,
Not knowing what horror was down in the deep.
She cut through the water, a near perfect dive,
And thought herself lucky to still be alive.

With no time to waste now she opened her eyes,
And what she saw gave her an awful surprise.
A world that stretched beyond what she could dream.
That begged every bit of her body to scream.

Beyond monsters were mountains and further still past
There floated more worlds with each worse than the last.
As madness took over, she closed her eyes tight.
Then she turned herself 'round with all of her might.

She looked once again and saw the split stone
Beyond which the world she'd known as her own.
Nightmares and monsters closed in on her fast,
All from a terrible universe vast.

She gripped the stone halves with one in each hand,
And pushed them together just as she'd planned,
And when she came back up, much to her pleasure,
Her plan had succeeded by every measure.

The water was churning as she stood in wonder.
As terrible creatures were being pulled under.
The sun had now risen and brought with it light
And also, an end to the terrible night.

At the edge of the pool, she stood all alone.
Gripped in her hand the mysterious stone.
And Dani just watched, with a smile as she wept,
As the horrors were summoned back into the depth.

You Brave Souls

Could you see through the darkness
or swim through the tears?
Could you swallow your screams
or silence your fears?

Could you steel yourself
from the madness of sorrow?
If you knew only pain
could you wake up tomorrow?

Would you lay down and die
If left all alone?
Could you manage a smile
If all on your own?

Brave souls, when you're drowning
Neck deep in despair,
Do nothing but fight
for each small breath of air.

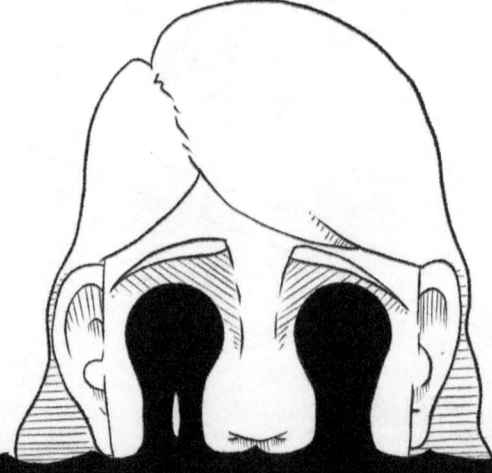

So, you've managed to make it through my new, even spookier, book? You certainly are a brave one.

This revised version used A.I. to produce the new images along with some digital editing by me to fix many of the A.I. mistakes. While I did my fair share of touch-ups, A.I. did the heavy lifting. I'm absolutely terrified by how much better it is than us at things, but also excited. The work it was able to produce brought my vision much closer to it's original intent. Something my drawing skills just couldn't do.

I've also included some blank pages so you can write you're own scary poems!

Thanks for reading!

www.ingramcontent.com/pod-product-compliance
Lightning Source LLC
Chambersburg PA
CBHW022027170626
46808CB00003B/1089